10

J
Sargent

Dan

By

Dave and Pat Sargent

Illustrated by
Jane Lenoir

Ozark Publishing, Inc.
P.O. Box 228
Prairie Grove, AR 72753

Sargent, Dave, 1941-
    Dan / by Dave and Pat Sargent ; illustrated by Jane
Lenoir. — Prairie Grove, AR : Ozark Publishing, ©2001.
    ix, 36 p. : col. ill. ; 23 cm.   (Saddle-up series)

    "Determination"—Cover.
    SUMMARY: A dappled mahogany bay horse proves his
loyalty as he carries Paul Revere through the countryside to
alert patriots that the British are coming. Includes factual
information on bay horses.
    ISBN: 1-56763-651-9   (hc)
             1-56763-652-7 (pbk)

    1. Revere, Paul, 1735-1818—Juvenile fiction. [1. Revere,
Paul, 1735-1818—Fiction. 2. Loyalty—Fiction.
3. Horses—Fiction. 4. United States—History—Revolution,
1775-1783—Fiction.]   I. Sargent, Pat, 1936-   II. Lenoir,
Jane, 1950-   ill. III. Title. IV. Series.

    PZ10.3. S243Dan 2001
    [E]—dc21   2001-002602

Printed in the United States of America

Inspired by

the beautiful dappled mahogany bays we see as we travel from state to state. Their coat has a lot of red in it, and they look so shiny. There are black tips on the red hairs, and sometimes black hairs mixed in with the red hairs. We have also seen those with brown manes and tails. At times we have to slow down and look close at the croup and withers to be able to see the dapples.

Dedicated to

everyone who loves horses. If you have a horse, take care of it daily. Horses are proud animals.

Foreword

One day, if you haven't already, you will study about the midnight ride of Paul Revere. His faithful steed was a beautiful dappled mahogany bay by the name of Dan.

Three horses and three men made history the night they raced across the countryside sounding the alarm, **"The British are coming**!**"**

Dan ran and ran until he was all lathered up and ready to drop, but he kept going. He loved life and knew he had to do his part to save this new country from British rule.

The ride was successful and had just ended when a British soldier stepped out of the darkness and said, "Halt!"

Contents

Dan

If you would like to have the authors of the Saddle Up Series visit your school, free of charge, call 1-800-321-5671 or 1-800-960-3876.

One

The British Are Coming!

The full moon cast shadows beneath the trees, and a coyote shared his mournful howl with the starlit heavens. Dan the dappled mahogany bay was not aware of the beauty or of nature's song as he raced down the road from Concord toward Lexington. The muscles in his legs and shoulders strained against the determined effort with each stride. His breath was coming in short gasps. Talk to me, Boss, he thought. You don't normally wake

1

me in the middle of the night to run
footraces across the country.

A sharp bend in the road caused him to suddenly change leads.

"Boss," he gasped, "I don't know where we are going or why we are in such a big hurry, but I know you have a good reason."

Five minutes later, the dappled mahogany bay was reined to a halt in front of a large white house. Dan took a deep breath and snorted as Paul Revere leaped from his back and ran to the front door.

He pounded on it with his fists, yelling, "Wake up, John Hancock! I have to talk to you." Moments later, a man appeared in the doorway yawning. He was barefoot, and the sleeping cap on his head hung limply over one eye. He straightened it.

"I am not the only one confused about my boss's strange behavior,"

Dan chuckled. "This poor fellow thinks he's having a nightmare!"

Paul Revere paced back and forth in front of John as he explained his actions.

"John, General Thomas Gage, the British military governor of Massachusetts, has issued a warrant to arrest you and Samuel Adams," he said. "He also intends to take all of the military supplies stored by the Whig party at Concord."

"Oh," Dan murmured. "Now I understand the importance of our fast ride through the night."

As the front door closed, Paul went back to the dappled mahogany bay and stroked his lathered neck with one hand.

"Forgive me for working you so hard," he said quietly. "You will have a chance to rest a minute while John gets ready to ride with us."

"Thanks, Boss," Dan wheezed. "I don't like to complain, but I was getting pretty tired."

Within a short time, Dan was joined by a red roan.

"What's going on?" the horse asked in a gruff voice. "My boss has lost his mind! No horse with any sense runs around at this time of night." He glared at Dan before adding, "Except some nut like you."

"Humph," Dan snorted. "Boss and I are trying to save your oats, buddy. And you are going to help."

The ride to Samuel Adams's home was only a short distance, but the red roan was panting as they stopped in front of his house.

"It looks like you need to do this more often," Dan chuckled. "Too many oats. Too little exercise."

The red roan glared at him, but he did not deny Dan's comment. Soon the dappled mahogany bay and red roan were joined by a sleepy lobo dun.

"What are we doing up at this time of night?" the lobo dun asked.

The dappled mahogany bay pawed the ground with his front hoof and said, "We are making history, fellows. Our bosses are getting ready to form a new nation."

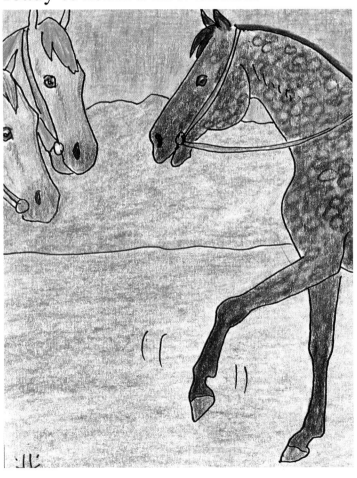

"What do you mean by that?" the red roan asked.

"I mean this country is about to break away from British rule," he explained. "If they are successful, this country will be her own boss."

"Wow!" the red roan and the lobo dun exclaimed in unison. "This is important stuff!"

Three horses and three men raced through the night. Their very important mission was to pass the troubling news of the British plans to confiscate the military supplies.

Finally slowing down to a trot, the dappled mahogany bay nodded his head and snorted, "I'm sorry, Boss. I wish I wouldn't ever get tired. This struggle to change leadership is so important to the folks in this country."

Paul patted him on the neck and whispered, "You're doing a fine job, Dan. You just be ready to run when I need your help, okay?"

"Sure, Boss," Dan murmured. "You can count on me."

Two

One if by Land . . .

The sun was peeking over the eastern horizon as the horses and their bosses came to a halt in front of a store. After tying the reins to a hitching post, the bosses disappeared within the building.

"Is this what your boss does to make money?" the red roan asked. "Who does he work for?"

Dan chuckled and said, "No, Boss doesn't get paid for running around all night and getting folks out of bed. He's a silversmith."

"Oh," the red roan replied. "Mine is a politician. Silversmith sounds more exciting. What is it?"

"Well, he makes and engraves and sells silver things like sugar bowls and tankards," Dan explained. "He's the best silversmith in the country." He hesitated a moment before adding in a strong, proud voice, "No. I take that back. He is the best silversmith in the whole wide world!"

Suddenly the door of the store opened, and the three bosses walked toward the hitching post where Dan and the other two were waiting.

"Okay, Paul," Samuel Adams said. "Let me make sure I understand your signals. If the British are approaching by sea, you will have two lanterns. Right?"

"Right, Sam," Paul Revere replied with a nod of his head. "I will expose two lanterns in Boston's North Church steeple if British ships are coming. If they arrive by land, I will have only one lantern in my hand. Spread the word among the patriots."

"We'll do that right away," John Hancock assured him. "We'll be ready to defend our cause."

Two days later on April 18, 1775, Dan was calmly eating hay when his boss hurried into his stall.

"Okay, Dan," he said, "it's time for us to go to work."

Dan took a deep breath and nodded his head.

"I'm rested, ready, and raring to go, Boss," he said.

A moment later, the boss of the

slate grullo in the stall next to Dan entered the stable. The slate grullo looked at Dan with raised eyebrows.

"Hmmm," he muttered. "It looks like I have to go to work, too. This is a strange hour to start a day. The sun is going down instead of coming up. That's kind of backward, isn't it?"

"That depends," Dan said with a little chuckle. "If your boss is as versatile as mine, there's no telling what or when things will happen."

Paul shook the hand of the man and smiled. "It's time to begin our ride, William Dawes. Are you ready to write a new chapter in history?"

"I sure am," William replied. "My slate grullo and I will go the Boston Neck route."

"Right," Paul Revere agreed.

"And Dan and I will go by way of Charleston and tell all the folks that the British are coming."

"Wow!" Dan exclaimed. "This is it. This is the news everyone has been expecting and preparing for." He took a deep breath and added, "Okay, Boss. I'm ready to run."

Ten minutes later, Dan and his boss took the north fork in the road as the slate grullo and his boss veered down the south fork.

"Dan and I will meet you in Lexington," Paul yelled. "We must hurry!"

The sound coming from the running slate grullo was lost amid the thundering hooves of Dan as he stretched his stride to the maximum. His boss leaned over his neck and spoke encouraging words as they raced through the night.

Pausing in front of each patriot's house, Dan waited as Paul Revere shouted, "The British are coming!"

They waited only long enough to hear voices from within the house acknowledging the warning. Then the dappled mahogany bay and his silversmith boss continued their journey toward the home of the next patriot. Hmmm, Dan thought as he raced across a small wooden bridge, I truly believe this is one night I'll never forget!

Three

Under Arrest

The sky in the east was just beginning to cast light upon the land as Dan the dappled mahogany bay and Paul Revere entered the town of Lexington. The horse was lathered and breathing hard, and the man looked exhausted. Dan skidded to a halt beside the slate grullo, the red roan, and the lobo dun. His boss leaped from his back and ran inside the building.

"Wow!" the roan exclaimed. "You look a mess."

"You don't look so good your-self," Dan snorted. He looked at the slate grullo and growled. "Did you stop at the homes of all the patriots on your route?"

"We sure did," he replied. "But I honestly don't think we had as many miles to travel as you and your boss."

"Well, guys," Dan said slowly, "my work is about done for the day. But," he paused and pointed a hoof toward the four men walking toward them, "yours has just begun."

Paul Revere shook the hand of each one.

"Good luck on your journey to Woburn," he said. "We are united in our quest to eliminate the British rule in this untamed land. Just be alert for British interference. They will stop us from forming a new nation if they can."

Dan yawned and shook his body. "And," he mumbled, "I wish you three horses good luck, too."

The slate grullo, the red roan, and the lobo dun laughed as Dan's voice drifted into a gentle snore.

"You should not laugh at Dan," Charles Dawes said. "We are going to Concord, and you other two are going to Woburn."

"Uh oh," the red roan groaned.

"May I please have the day off, Boss?" the lobo dun asked quietly.

"I'm too old for this business," the slate grullo complained. "Don't you think I should be retired, Boss?"

Of course, the groans, moans, and complaints of the three horses fell on deaf ears. A moment later, the red roan, Boss Samuel Adams, the lobo dun, Boss John Hancock, the slate grullo, and Boss Charles Dawes were ready to travel. Paul gently untied the dappled mahogany bay from the hitching post.

Minutes later, Samuel Adams and John Hancock were racing down the street and soon disappeared from view.

"Come on, Dan," Paul said.

The dappled mahogany bay opened an eye and nodded his head.

"What now, Boss? We have spread the word. The other folks can take care of those British fellows."

Suddenly a British officer with a musket in one hand appeared on the street. His voice echoed against the stillness of early morning.

"Halt!"

He questioned Charles Dawes and Paul Revere for several minutes. Then he motioned for the slate grullo and Charles to leave.

"Uh oh," Dan groaned. "It looks like Boss may be in trouble."

"Everything will be okay, Dan," Paul whispered. "They won't keep me locked up for long, and it will give you a chance to rest."

Dan nodded his head, but a tear slowly slid down his cheek.

"This won't amount to anything but a short visit with the British," Paul assured him. "And then you and I can travel the countryside in this new nation of freedom together. We'll have lots of fun times!"

Dan smiled and nickered softly. "Okay, Boss. Enjoy your short stay with the British. I'll rest up a bit."

Hmmm, Dan thought as he watched Boss walk away with the officer. I know in my heart this new nation will always remember and appreciate Paul Revere. Maybe some fellow will even write a poem about him. And I wonder if they'll remember the dappled mahogany bay who carried Paul Revere safely through the darkness of the night. It's not important. I'll wait here for Boss, and then my life will be great!

Four

Dappled Mahogany Bay Facts

Bays are horses with bodies that are some shade of red. All bays have black points.

Dappling refers to the dark areas that lay over lighter areas on the horse.

Sometimes there are differences in the hair of various areas of the skin, so dapples can be seen even on black horses. *Dappling* is most noticeable when horses shed, or change coats, in the spring and fall.

Mahogany bays are sometimes

referred to as *dark bay* and come from black hairs being mixed into the red body coat. This is noticed most over the croup and withers.

Black points can be individual black hairs or black tips on the red hairs. Even on some mahogany bays with black points, the mane and tail can fade to brown.

All *bays* have red in their coat, and this gives the coat a brilliance and sheen. This makes the dapples on the coat really show up on the *dappled mahogany bay*.